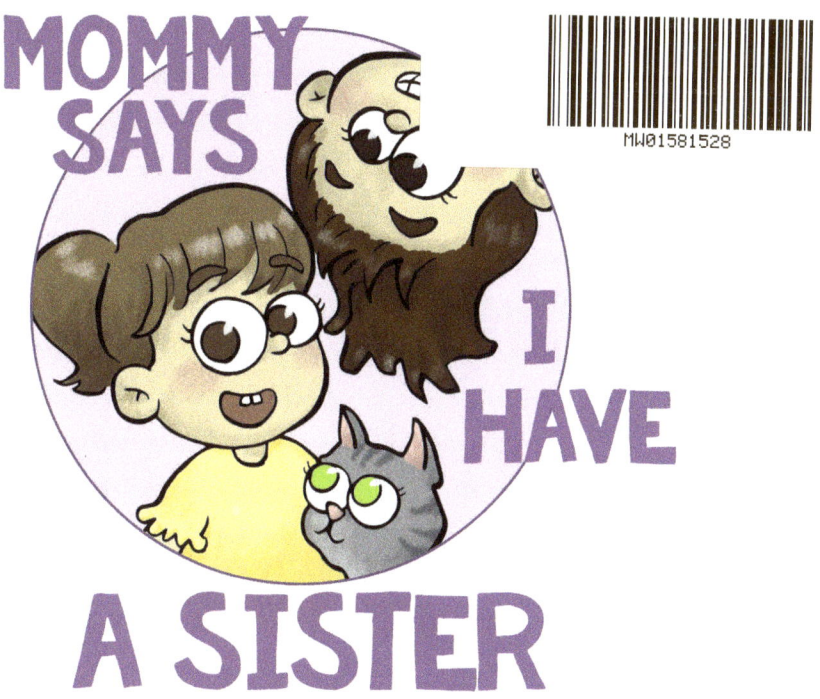

*In loving memory of my sweet boy, Grayson.
You have taught me to hug tighter, laugh louder and love deeper.*

*To the stars and back,
Mommy*

Copyright © 2020 Stephany Resendes
Published by Iguana Books
720 Bathurst Street, Suite 303
Toronto, Ontario, Canada M5S 2R4
All rights reserved.
ISBN: 978-1-77180-469-1
Book design and front cover image: Kerry Bell
This is an original print edition of
Mommy Says I Have A Sister.

IGUANA

She's THERE when I need a FRIEND or someone to HOLD me TIGHT

Mommy says you're WITH ME when I'm HAPPY or I'm SAD

In MY HEART you're always there — That, FOR SURE, I know

She TALKS about you ALL the time (She might be YOUR biggest FAN.)

Mommy even tells me that we'll GET TO MEET someday

Until we do,
my SISTER and
FRIEND,
In my
HEART
you'll
stay

CPSIA information can be obtained
at www.ICGtesting.com
Printed in the USA
BVHW020146250321
603374BV00003B/9